IT'S RAINING UNDER THE F***ING SKY

DEVMALYA GHOSH

Dedicated to Baba and his first love

Contents

Acknowledgements *vii*

1. It's Raining Under The F***ing Sky 1

It's Your Story Too 7

Acknowledgements

Acknowledging the current situation

CHAPTER ONE

It's raining under the F***ing sky

Teen age is what will put you in complexes. And this age usually taught us what life is, and how to deal with it. Though it is tough , because no one will teach you how to overcome it. And how to fight with it. Not even your parents. Yes it's that much fucking hard.

I'm also not an exception in this case. This age through me and again holds my hands. And right now I'm writing my fucking story. How much I can remember about that day is
it's heavily raining in Rajarhat (A small town near kolkata) . I've never liked to go to tuition classes.
Especially if it is history class. But neighbours are god , one of my neighbours influenced my mother to put me in that class. God cannot convince your mother but neighbours can. If they're saying The sun Raises in the west My maa will believe that. And if I'm saying no maa it's wrong she will slap on my face . I don't have that much guts to take my mom's hard hands slap so in this type of situation usually I prefer being silent.

Alas! I took admission. On the very first day when I entered that class the room was full of students, and only one place was blank . The teacher told me to sit there. I was feeling really occurred at that moment. The seat is in the corner . I'm not hesitating because the seat is in the corner , I was feeling that it occurred because a girl is sitting over there . Don't think I'm a fool or something because at that time I was fourteen years old .

After seeing my hesitation my super pro I mean to say my ultra max pro teacher said - " why are you feeling shy ? Ha ha ha she is your friend".

Huh! If i can understand this friendship will fucked me up . I'll never sit over there what ever after one or two months I've left that tution by grace of god (neighbours) .

Hustle is actually part of our life, After giving my 10th grade board exam, it should be named as a bored exam . What ever I've passed out that exam with ? Any guesses? No, you are wrong I've passed out that exam by holding 40 % marks clap for me please. Actually my maa should clap and she does that also by using her one hand one pair of shoes and my back. I think everything is completed but my very special relatives are very supportive . They convince not only my mom but also my father to add some salt in this special segment. They are supportive for my maa not for me . If you are thinking they're supportive for me then you are stupid10 × Foolish90

=> 10× stupid × 90 × foolish

=> -90× Foolish × - 10 × stupid

=> Youu are fuckinggggggg dumb

{ Don't try to understand this math try to understand my emotions}

=> You = Foolish (proved)

After almost 10 months my father was in our place after knowing my results from the UK.

And said " baba I've never expected this thing, just for you

I've come from uttarakhand.
I replied - " oh I think you are coming from the United Kingdom " .
The next day me and baba visited a mall to buy a new leather belt for him.
Now the time is for admission in school. Again that ultra max pro neighbours and my relatives influenced my baba to convince me to take commerce as my stream for +2 .
Ha ha I've never like to read history books and now this is the chance , and I've taken that . Who knows there is a subject called business studies.

What ever I'm in my class 11 which is the most important thing.
Time for flying and flewed alot in this time more then a bird i guess. Never open first page of a study book also.
Dated one girl then we broke up . Then again I've started finding a new girl, I should proud of me . How much patianate I am. At that time I'm in girls girls and girls too many girls. But life is unpredictable and the most unpredictable mind changing age group is teen age. When your maturity level heats you , you can't understand thay.

And the most over rated myth is you know everything . What ever now the time for half yearly exam from 40% bellow avarage student I've become a topper with 98% marks . And become crush of the school.
What ever i dont want to be a play boy or something. I just want to be in a relationship. With a girl to whom i can share everything. My happiness to frustration. Last but not lust i want to share my love .
Usually what we want in our life god denied that or scream loudly on us and says fuck off.
But in this case I'm the exception.
Shefali came in my life . That girl with whom my ultra max

pro teacher says to sit . I've never thought she'll be mine. 5"3 , Dark , Indian beauty with pure soul. Usually when ever walk in a road my fucking friends look at us and sing a hindi song " Rab ne banadi Jodi " .... I don't know rab ever tried to do that or not but always they want me and shefali to be in a relationship.

Our relationship is never like hookups and all. We are friends best friends of each other who can give life too .

I'm that person who did every mistakes in his life. Once of her friend nisha was close to me . And me and shefali always had a fight with each other. Usually it's sustaind till 3 to 4 days . But this time it's extended till 1 month . I've proposed nisha because i want she should jalous it's her punishment. I knew that nisha and shefali are not talking with each other. So that's a plus point. I'll get my attention and she'll be jalous also. But some time we've make fool our self only.

After this bull shit when we are again back to our zone . Suddenly I've received a text on what's app from shefali

- good

I knew that I've did a blunder. So when shefalis 2 friends call me I didn't say a single word . I've sturted felling Numb

.

I've said to my self " you are fuckedup and who did this sit you only you .

Next day at eve I've checked my phone at 3.30 PM and it's visible on screen - 2 missed calls from shefali . Again ph started ringng and I've recieved a text

- pickup my phone

I've replied - I can't

- I'm sorry

Shefali says

- i don't want to take this shits pickup my call.

I've replied - please leave it.
After maximum 2 seconds, she replied.
- I'm saying please
Then again she texted and says " promise me whatever I'll ask you, you will answer the truth only ? "

I've replied - promise
- those screenshots are real or not ? I can believe it's you?

I've lost my words . How much faith this girl has on me.
I've replied yes
She says - swear on me
I've says- swear on you.

She replied you've stoll my arrogance. At that day I've lost not only her, I've lost my self and it's raining under the fucking sky . From two places from our eyes.

It's Your Story Too

More volumes will come. It's a story where you can find yourself your own story . It's not only my story it's your story too.

The End

www.ingramcontent.com/pod-product-compliance
Lightning Source LLC
Chambersburg PA
CBHW022048150726
47990CB00004B/1653

* 9 7 9 8 8 8 7 7 2 6 2 1 2 *